Arctic State

A Constable David Maratse stand-alone novella
set in Greenland

CHRISTOFFER PETERSEN

Don't miss the second instalment

Arctic Rebel

Arctic State

By Christoffer Petersen

AARLUUK PRESS

ISBN: 978-87-93680-75-3

www.christoffer-petersen.com

Location
Location
Location

CHRISTOFFER PETERSEN

Real People
not
Real Estate

Arctic State

The Office of Intermediary Greenlandic Affairs

They had a name for it – the Office of Intermediary Greenlandic Affairs. The staff who worked there called it the IGA. The Greenlanders didn't call it anything. Most of them didn't know that it existed, nor *where* it existed. It could have been in a different place, a different time even. But its existence was *here* and *now*, tucked away in a large, and yet altogether unassuming square building close to the airport in Nuuk, overlooking the extended and improved runway. The line of communication from Washington D.C. to the IGA was, by Arctic standards, free of static and wholly unaffected by fading – the atmospheric anomaly that plagued satellite communications in the far north. In other words, access to the White House was immediate, emphasising the new-found status of the world's largest island as the jewel in the proverbial crown of the republic of the United States of America. The IGA was on the inside, kept in the national security loop, and very much charged with the purpose of bolstering the strategic buffer that Greenland was, in the intense and often churlish quest of both Arctic and near-

Arctic states to dominate the region. The IGA had departments and offices for every aspect of Greenlandic affairs, from overseeing the installation of defensive missile batteries – the Arctic equivalent of the Patriot – to the quiet and determined work of the staff responsible for the relocation of the Greenlanders. The resettlement plan, practiced in all secrecy by the Greenlandic government prior to America's interest and subsequent purchase of Greenland, focused on moving Greenlanders from the remote settlements and villages to the main towns and the capital city of Nuuk. The plan called for depopulating the north, emptying the east and closing the ludicrously expensive transport network to all but the IGA administration, visiting dignitaries and the richest of tourists. Such work was deemed vital if the costs of acquiring the new colony were to be kept in budget, proportionate to the population, with as much respect and concern for the culture, tradition and languages of the people as the purse-holders could stomach. Separating and absorbing the Greenlandic police from the Danish government was an integral part of the relocation plan. For the plan to run smoothly, as smoothly as it possibly could in such a harsh environment, the full cooperation of the Greenlandic police was considered tantamount to success. Therefore, when dissidents or uncooperative members of the police force – including officers and administrative staff – were identified, they were called in by the IGA department for the Naturalisation of Indigenous

Assets for a quiet chat. Greenland officially became the 51st of the United States, six months after the initial handover date, trumping the beleaguered residents of Puerto Rico simply because of Greenland's position in the world. Constable David Maratse was invited for his first chat exactly one month later.

The following account is based on the official transcripts of Constable David Maratse's interviews, together with supplemental background information from eyewitnesses, national and international media coverage, rumour, speculation and gossip.

Part 1

Summer in the capital of Nuuk. Constable David Maratse stopped for coffee at the newly opened drive-thru with the large neon back-lit sign that advertised coffee at all hours. He stared up at the sign from the window of the patrol car. It obscured the view of the mountains in the near distance, as did the touch-screen menu that prompted him to *go large*, to *add more*, complicating the simple act of buying a simple coffee. There were rumours of a McDonalds to be built in the dirt along the main road to the airport, and another closer to the centre of the city. Maratse tapped the minus symbol several times until he was ready to purchase a single cup of black coffee – no milk, no sugar, no cake by the side. He selected the cash option and drove to the window to pay. They were still accepting Danish kroner – coins and notes – although the media was full of the imminent change to dollars, and what it meant for the average Greenlander. Maratse paid for his coffee, drove to the second window to collect it, and then stuffed the cup into the holder to the right of the police radio. He removed the lid to let it cool as he drove; the coffee steamed all the way to the airport.

Maratse showed his police identity card at the security gate guarding the entrance to the IGA building next to the airport terminal. He waited for the guard to check his name on the list of visitors, tried a sip of coffee, before returning it to the holder to cool. The guard waved him through a few seconds later. Maratse parked the tiny patrol car between two large, black SUVs. He left the coffee in the car as he walked to the entrance.

They checked his identity card a second time at the security booth just inside the door. He unbuckled his utility belt and left it in one of the secure lockers, signing for it with a thumbprint on a tablet, and then removed his jacket for the pat-down.

"That could do with a wash," the guard said, pointing at Maratse's jacket as soon as he was finished with the search. Maratse shrugged and took a seat in the waiting area.

Special Assistant Spenser Walcott entered the waiting area from the middle door of three at the back of the room, opposite the secure entrance. He strode across the floor, welcomed Maratse with a firm handshake, and then gestured for Maratse to follow him.

"We're just along the hall," he said, swiping his identity card through the card reader by the side of the door. He turned the handle as soon as the alarm buzzed. "Do you want coffee? Breakfast? How about some juice?"

"Coffee," Maratse said. He looked at the rows

of desks tucked into cubicles, two-deep, on the right side of the room, until Walcott showed him into the last of four offices on the left. The buzz of activity from the cubicles hushed to a whisper, as Walcott shut the office door and pointed at the chair on the far side of a round table. He poured two mugs of coffee from a thermos can as Maratse sat down.

"It's good that you could come in so soon," Walcott said, as he handed Maratse his coffee. "I wasn't sure we would meet before August." He sat down, taking a quick slurp before opening the folder in front of him. "Normally, this would all be digital, but I had this prepared in the event that I had to come to you." He smiled. "Can't trust the Internet on the east coast – at least, that's what they tell me."

"*Iiji.*" Maratse said.

"Ah, I'm sorry, it's just English. Is that okay with you? They told me you could speak English, but if you need a translator…"

"I can speak English."

"Good." Walcott spread the first few papers from the folder on the table between them. He tugged a pen from the breast pocket of his shirt and clicked the nib ready for writing. "As you know," he said, eyes down as he scanned the papers. "We're pulling in nearly all of your colleagues for what we call the 360."

"*Nearly* all my colleagues."

"That's right," Walcott said. "The ones we're not letting go."

"Letting go where?"

"Sorry?"

"Where are they going?" Maratse asked.

"It's an expression," Walcott said. He waited for Maratse to nod that he understood, before continuing with a sigh when he didn't. "It's another way of saying they were fired."

"For what?"

Walcott clicked his pen as he studied Maratse's face. "That's confidential," he said. "Can we move on?"

"*Iiji.*"

Another click of the pen. Walcott made a note on the line beside the list of checkboxes on one of the sheets of paper.

"See, that's not very helpful, Constable. I said you would need to speak English." He looked up. "And you replied that you could – speak English. Which is it?"

"I can speak English," Maratse said. He took a sip of coffee, thought of the coffee cooling in the car, and of the drive-thru sign obscuring the mountains. It struck him then that the office had no windows, not unless you counted the thin frame of thick glass in the door.

"Then we'll move on." Walcott smiled. "No harm done." He put his pen down and picked up the first sheet of paper. "This is standard procedure," he said. "The integration of the Greenlandic Police Force into the United States criminal justice system is proving to be a bit of a hurdle. I'm sure you can appreciate that. However, these 360s…"

"What's that?"

"A 360?" Walcott paused. "Well, it's another way of saying we're looking at the whole picture, a detailed review of each police officer and administrative employee."

"What are you looking for?"

"Everything and nothing," Walcott said. He tried a smile to lighten the mood but shook it off when Maratse failed to reciprocate. "Let's just say we're looking for the right fit. This is very new, for all of us. It's important to get things right, to make sure we're all on the same page, from day one." He shuffled the papers and pulled another from the folder. "We have a basic checklist that gives us an initial idea about who we can or can't work with. We put this together based on markers from personnel records, together with a written statement from three sources providing a deeper insight about the employee's character. In your case," he said, "the references are overwhelmingly positive. But..."

"But?"

"The markers, Constable, are counter indicative."

Maratse frowned. "I don't understand. *Markers*?"

"Things we flag in a file."

"Flag?"

Walcott sighed as he tapped the edges of the papers into a single pile in front of him. "It means we underline things that we find interesting, or maybe even alarming."

"Counter indicative?"

"Of being the right fit, yes," Walcott said.

"Frankly, Constable, your file was full of them."

"Flags?"

"And markers. You have a most interesting background, and a lot of history." Walcott picked up his pen, clicked the nib into position and pressed it to the first line next to the list of checkboxes. "How about you answer some questions, and we can take it from there?"

"*Iiji,*" Maratse said. He looked directly at Walcott, waiting for him to begin.

"Yeah, I'm going to let that go." He took a sip of coffee before the first question. "How would you describe yourself?"

"What?"

"Let's see." Walcott tapped the nib of his pen on the paper. "Do you consider yourself Greenlandic?"

Maratse nodded.

"And are you a patriot?"

"In what way?"

"For example, how do you celebrate Greenland's National Day – June 21?" Walcott waited a beat, waited for Maratse, then continued, "Do you celebrate with friends? Attend local events, maybe watch them on television?"

"I don't have a television."

"Okay, but if you did, would you watch these events?"

"No."

"Because they're not important?"

"Because I don't watch television."

"Yes, we've established that you don't have a television, Constable, but…"

"If I was working, I would go to an event."

"For work, then. Not pleasure? Not in your spare time?"

"I hunt in my spare time."

"Okay then," Walcott said. He made a series of quick notes, looking up as Maratse leaned forwards to read what he had written. "I've put you down as *passive*," he said. "A passive patriot."

"What's that?"

"Someone who doesn't celebrate, most likely someone who doesn't care."

"About my country?"

"Yes, someone who doesn't care about Greenland." Walcott raised his hands, dipping his palms up and down like a weighing scale. "Someone who doesn't love it but doesn't hate it either. You're passive. Non-active."

"I care for my country."

"Yes, but you don't feel the need to celebrate it."

"No. Not on television."

"Or in any way whatsoever."

"I hunt."

"That's hardly celebrating."

"But it's Greenlandic," Maratse said. "What does this have to do with my job?"

Walcott ignored Maratse as he made a few rough notes. When he was finished, he put down his pen, leaned his elbows on the table and steepled his fingers, staring at Maratse over the top of them.

"These questions – of which this is the first –

allow us to fill in the blanks, and, in your case, enable us to get an idea of who you are, the man between the markers and the statements."

"I don't understand the markers," Maratse said. "What have you *flagged*?"

"*Flagged*? It's interesting," Walcott said. "Suddenly you can conjugate verbs?"

"Tell me about the markers?"

Walcott shuffled more papers out of the folder, until he had a fan of documents spread between him and Maratse.

"This marker," he said, pointing at a paragraph of text highlighted in yellow, "concerns repeated incidents where you disobeyed orders, or took matters into your own hands, often shanghaiing civilians to assist you…"

"I work in the settlements. There aren't many people around to help."

"And yet, you compromise operational integrity, and put lives at risk, including your own. Someone who does that, repeatedly, is not a good fit for us."

"They would be counter inductive?"

"Yes," Walcott sighed. "That's exactly what they would be."

"And you would have to let them go?"

"Yes." Walcott frowned as Maratse pushed back his chair to stand up. "Where are you going?"

"I thought you were letting me go?"

"Constable," he said. "I can't figure you out. Either you understand English, or you don't. I don't know how much plainer I can make this."

"You're not letting me go?"

"No. Not at this moment."

"But I'm not a good fit."

"To be honest, Constable, you're a terrible fit. You have a history of reckless action, across the whole of Greenland, identified here," Walcott said, stabbing his finger on the highlighted text. "And here." Another piece of paper. "Here and here." Walcott tapped the folder, suggesting there were even more counter inductive markers inside. "But the statements about your character do not match your written record. How do you explain that, Constable?"

Maratse shrugged. "Sometimes you just have to act."

"And yet, some of those *acts* have led you on chases – manhunts, for want of a better word – without backup, or worse, together with civilians, and, sometimes, together with the suspect, or others directly associated with the case. It's like you can't distance yourself from your people, which, frankly, makes it very difficult for us to trust you will do the right thing when we ask you to."

"The right thing?"

"Yes."

"How would I know?"

"Know what?"

"If what you wanted me to do was the right thing?"

"Because we would tell you." Walcott frowned. "Surely you understand that?"

"It would depend on the situation," Maratse

said.

"And that's where we get into difficulty." Walcott stood up and picked up a laptop computer from the docking station on a counter against the wall. He brought it to the table, opened the lid, and turned the screen towards Maratse. "Do you recognise this woman?"

Maratse looked at the image of an older, black-haired Greenlandic woman, her face twisted as she tried to break free of the grip of two American security personnel. He recognised the background as the security area of Kangerlussuaq International Airport.

"That's Inniki Rasmussen," Maratse said.

"That's right. Quite a spry woman for her age. Seventy-one," Walcott said. "According to our records." He turned the laptop to open a file on the screen. "This was taken with a security camera, on the day that Ms. Rasmussen resisted our attempts to question her on her arrival at the airport. I believe she had just returned from a two-week visit to Denmark."

"*Iiji*," Maratse nodded.

"Apparently Ms. Rasmussen had some objections to a number of new initiatives designed to improve the welfare of Greenlanders across the country, which resulted in her being apprehended by airport security – following a heated discussion with the security personnel." Walcott looked up from the laptop. "She was placed in your custody."

Maratse finished his coffee as Walcott stared at him. He glanced at the highlighted chunks of text on the pages spread in front of Walcott, counting seven before he put his mug down.

"Yes," he said.

"Did you know of Ms. Rasmussen's history prior to escorting her?"

"A little."

"And yet, you resisted the team that was assigned to you to help bring her in."

"She's an older woman," Maratse said. "They were unnecessary."

"Really? How about we talk to your Police Commissioner, down at the station?" Walcott said, pointing at the wall in what might have been the general direction of the city centre, if only there had been windows to confirm it.

Maratse shrugged. "I made a decision. The situation developed."

"I'll say it did, Constable. Which is why you're 360 has been bumped up to today. This could be your last day on the force, Constable. You might even face criminal charges. So, might I suggest that you take a more proactive role in this meeting, start volunteering your answers, without me having to drag them out of you, and tell me what the hell happened in Kapisillit."

Part 2

Inniki Rasmussen had missed the first wave of protests railing against the United States' purchase of Greenland. The medical staff at *Rigshopitalet* on Blegdamsvej, Denmark, had quietly removed the remote for the television in her room, disconnected the radio, and all but covered the windows – anything to ease her pain and speed her recovery. The doctors all agreed that the myomectomy procedure to remove fibroids in Inniki's uterus had been successful, but shadows of the pain prior to the operation returned during post-op recovery. Inniki wanted nothing to do with anyone or anything – *at all*. She would join the fight for her country, just as soon as she was fighting fit. At one time, such a thought might have made her smile, *but the pain –* she had to prioritise. When the doctors were ready to release Inniki, confident that she had made as thorough a recovery as could be expected for a woman of her age, arrangements were made for her return flight to Greenland.

It should have been a straightforward matter, and it used to be, with the Greenlandic government footing the bill for healthcare and the associated cost of transport, but nothing was straightforward anymore.

"We can put you on a flight," the nurse said, as she took Inniki's blood pressure, "but we don't know who's paying for it. There's a chance that you might get a bill."

"You mean I have to pay?"

"I'm not an expert. It's just what I've heard. It's what everybody is saying." The nurse waved a slight hand at the blank screen of the flat screen television mounted on the wall.

"It really happened then," Inniki said.

"Yes. I'm sorry." The nurse removed the Velcro sleeve from Inniki's arm, tidied away the blood pressure monitor, and quietly left the room.

Everyone was sorry.

The Danish media had been full of regret, including personal stories, profiles of professional Greenlanders choosing to leave their country and begin life in Denmark, as per the agreement hashed out in the boardrooms and backrooms of government offices in Copenhagen, Washington D.C., and even in Nuuk. But Nuuk was plagued with backlash, as recorded in features, double-spreads and supplements in the print media, together with in-depth interviews, amateur and activist reportage, blogs, columns, opinion pieces and all manner of social media. Greenland experienced a wave of international interest that reached beyond its melting glaciers when the American Commander-in-Chief revealed his interest in buying the country in a real estate deal, but it was nothing like the media frenzy that erupted when the first preliminary discussions were scheduled.

Like many Greenlanders, Inniki understood the need for someone – *anyone* – to invest in her country, but to buy it? No, she didn't understand that, she couldn't accept that, and neither, it seemed, could many of the Greenlanders who took to the streets on the official day when Greenland became a part of the United States. But like so many movements protesting the inevitable, once the deed was done, fewer remained to actively fight for its reversal. Within a month, even as the first changes began to be implemented and the second wave of American administrators arrived, the protesters had gone home, to the settlements and remote villages, to their families, hurrying back on the wave of a rumour of forced resettlement.

Inniki packed her bag, pausing for a breath in between, shifting her feet to find the best, most comfortable position to stand, then scolding herself for being so weak at a time when everyone needed to be strong. She slipped the small backpack over her shoulder and left the room, crossing the narrow corridor to the bathroom opposite. Inniki checked her hair in the mirror and smiled at the solitary strands of grey. She called them her *lightning streaks*, a sure sign that she was alive – charged even – that despite everything else, everything that was happening in the world – with *her* world, it was still turning, she was still aging, she was still alive. Such affirmation gave

Inniki an extra few centimetres. While others might baulk at the first sign of grey, she revelled in it, searching for more, accepting the change and embracing the next step of her journey in life.

"Onwards," she said, pressing her fingers into her creamy brown cheeks and letting go, measuring the elasticity with whispered counts of "*Ataaseq, marluk, pingasut...*" Her cheeks were paler now than they once were, but nothing a season on the ice would not cure. She let go of her cheeks, turned her wrinkled hands in the light from the mirror, smiled at the memory of holding the shaft of a dog whip in one hand, before frowning at the memory of holding a gun in the other. In truth, she realised, there had been fewer seasons on the ice, and far more seasons carrying a gun, for her country – both of them, acting on behalf of the Danish and, later, the Greenlandic governments. She had even worked for the Americans. "And now they're back," she said, with a last glance in the mirror before leaving the bathroom.

The nurses directed Inniki to the administration offices where they assured her, she would get answers, and a plane ticket home, maybe even later that day – so many people were cancelling their flights to Greenland.

"It's the unrest," the nurse said. "Nobody wants to go."

"Why?"

"Because of the unrest." The nurse shook her head in that quizzical way one does when someone is clearly out of the loop.

"I haven't been home for a while," Inniki said.

"But you're going to go back?"

"It's my home. Of course, I'm going back."

Inniki left the ward and took the elevator to the ground floor. She found the administrative offices, and a week's worth of newspapers on the coffee table in the waiting area. Inniki dumped her backpack into an empty chair, paused for a second as a wave of pain splintered through her body, then chose a sample of newspapers from the table. She read while she waited, wincing as the pain in her belly – and that deeper pain, the persistent one – fought for her attention, competing with the anger that bumped her blood pressure, surging through her veins to the very tips of her fingers. The images of young Greenlanders wearing masks on the streets, ducking canisters of tear gas that spiralled through the smoke of the capital, a torn Greenlandic flag, flaming at the edges, hanging from a street lamp, and the police patrol car burning outside the cultural centre *Katuaq*.

The price for regional stability in the Arctic, it seemed, was the destabilising of the country. Nuuk was burning, Greenland was hurting, and the winds of change were hurricane force. One of the largest countries in the world, with arguably the smallest population, smallest economy, and smallest expectations, was about to be consumed, eaten whole, swallowed by its North Atlantic neighbour turned master and administrator.

"Inniki Rasmussen?"

Inniki reacted the second time they called her name. She folded the newspapers, tucked them onto the table, and stood up. She wobbled as she reached for her backpack, shaking off the offer of assistance, and following the administrator back to her desk. Inniki listened as the woman ran through the available options – a flight the following day with one night at the Greenlanders' Patient Hotel, or a flight within the next few hours, if she hurried.

"That one," Inniki said.

The woman looked at her watch, the slim bracelet kind, and said, "You're sure?"

"I've been gone long enough. I need to get home."

"I understand." The woman made a call, booking Inniki onto the flight, arranging transport to the airport, before printing out all the details. "Keep this with you," she said, presenting Inniki with her boarding card. The woman held on for a second, waiting for Inniki to look at her. "I noticed the papers you were reading."

"Yes?"

"I am sorry. Truly sorry. I can't imagine..."

Nobody could, and least of all Inniki, although the thought of allowing herself to be the most affected – one way or another – was anathema to her. She shrugged it off as self-pity, something which she had no room for, as the only baggage listed on her ticket was carry-on. If it could fit in the overhead luggage compartment, she could take it with her. Pity, Inniki thought, was too big, too heavy, it only slowed you down and dulled your senses.

"And I need to be sharp," she whispered.

"What's that?" the woman asked.

"Nothing. *Qujanaq*."

Inniki walked out of the offices and along the hall to the main entrance. She found the patient transport ambulance just outside the door. The driver said they had to wait for more passengers but changed his mind when he saw Inniki's ticket.

"I'll come back for them," he said, ushering Inniki to her seat, before sliding the door to a close and climbing in behind the wheel. He chatted all the way to the airport, but Inniki said nothing, swapping the barest of glances, and the briefest of smiles until they arrived, and he escorted her to the check-in desk.

The Air Greenland assistant looked at Inniki, and said, "You're coming from the hospital. We can put you on one of our patient carts. Save you walking."

"I'd like that."

"You'll still have to go through security."

"I understand."

Security was always interesting, when the flags on Inniki's passport caught the attention of the security officers, raising an eyebrow just as they did for the assistant as she checked Inniki onto the flight. But Inniki couldn't remember ever being quite so disconcerted as when they waved her through with the briefest of comments about her identity. It was almost as if she was no longer their concern. They were sending her home. The Greenlanders and their new American masters could deal with Inniki Rasmussen.

She was tempted to resist the smooth course they had provided for her, to say something, to remind them that she was *the* Inniki Rasmussen who was connected to Eko Simigaq, if only to give them pause, to add a little turbulence to her passage through security. But she kept quiet, and the security staff did little more than confiscate her toothpaste – the family-sized tube she had bought the week before her operation.

"It's over one hundred millilitres," they said. "That's over 3.4 fluid ounces."

"What is?"

"The new measurement. It's the same, but new to you."

Inniki shook her head, not comprehending, blaming the pain in her stomach, wanting to sit down, then sitting on the electric cart that whizzed her to the gate, where they had begun boarding. Inniki was still wondering about security and fluid ounces as the flight attendants showed her to her seat, stuffed her backpack into the overhead locker, and brought her a glass of water so that she could take a painkiller. Inniki couldn't remember asking but realised the bottle of pills she had removed from her pack was a giveaway. She swallowed her pill and sipped her water until take-off.

She lost track of the first few hours, and it was only when Inniki finished her meal that she realised only half the seats in the cabin were occupied.

"You can sit in *Nanoq*, Business Class if

you'd be more comfortable," the attendant said.

"I'm all right."

"You're sure?"

Inniki took the attendant's hand as she turned to leave, and said, "Where is everyone?"

"You mean the passengers?"

"*Aap.*"

The attendant sighed, and said, "It's been like this for a few weeks now. The flights *out* of Greenland are full, although there are spaces next week."

"Why?"

"People are leaving. Those that can."

"They're moving to Denmark?"

"Yes."

"Permanently?"

The attendant nodded.

"What about you?" Inniki asked, suddenly aware of the flush of colour in the attendant's cheeks. "Are you leaving?"

"I've already left," she said. "How long have you been away?"

"A month."

"Things have changed. You'll see," the attendant said. She tried to smile as she backed away, but the truth lingered dully in her eyes.

"What kind of things?" Inniki asked, but the attendant was suddenly busy with another passenger. She caught Inniki's eye one last time before turning away. They didn't speak again.

Inniki gripped the arms of the chair when the pilot announced that they would be landing soon. Over the years, she had overcome her fear of flying, but the thought of bumping onto the runway and spurring another bout of pain sent her pulse racing.

The landing, however, was the smoothest part of her arrival at Kangerlussuaq International Airport, and the brief smile that creased her face at the first sight of the familiar mountains, evaporated as the flight attendant used the loudspeakers to inform passengers of the new arrivals procedure.

"All passengers are to remain seated, until instructed to do otherwise by an officer from the Office of Intermediary Greenlandic Affairs. Please, remain in your seats."

Inniki unbuckled her seatbelt and stood up.

Part 3

A warm wind followed the IGA officer into the aircraft, drifting along the aisle and over the seats of the cabin. Inniki caught the first scent of home – the tough Arctic grass and the dry earth. There was something else too, a sharper bite tumbling along inside the warmer air. It made Inniki think of glaciers and the thick, unyielding ice that covered almost all of her country. She planted her feet in the aisle – unyielding, but allowed herself a slight recompense, leaning her hip against the side of her seat as she bit back the stab of pain spreading from one hip to the other.

The IGA officer pointed at Inniki as he pressed the handset for the cabin speakers to the side of his face. "Ma'am," he said. "You need to take your seat." He waited for his Greenlandic assistant to translate, and then jabbed his fingers twice more at Inniki. "You need to sit down."

Inniki remained standing. In truth, it was better for her to stand than to sit, better for the pain, but she knew that even if she had been healthy, she would have stood up. It was important. She watched the IGA officer grow impatient, saw him nod to someone out of her view, and then heard the familiar tramp of heavy boots in a confined space. Inniki gripped the headrest of the seat as a man and a woman – Americans both – stomped towards her. They bristled with weapons of varying description, but the sharpest things about them were their tongues, plus the glint in their eyes that suggested time was short. It occurred to Inniki, as the two officers stepped into her personal space, that time in Greenland was both endless and finite, measured in degrees of light, gusts of wind, and changes in temperature. There was a time when the seasons were more defined, and time was measured accordingly, with certain jobs and tasks, travel even, influenced by the winds, the snows, the depth of the ice, the size of the waves. Time was just something that happened as a matter of course. It could be measured among Greenlanders in height, girth, wrinkles and the lightning streaks in Inniki's hair that she was so fond of. Time was not something to be forced or adjusted or even planned for. Sure, there were schedules and appointments to keep – flights and business meetings, for example. But even these were altered and adjusted by the wind, the waves, the...

Inniki lost the thread as the female officer stepped around her colleague and took Inniki's arm. Even that grip was enough to incite the pain in Inniki's uterus, her hips, her stomach, that band of her body that was still recovering. Inniki gasped, felt her cheeks pinch with the pain, heard the beginnings of an explanation – her own words

– as she tried to resist. She curled her hand around the cushion of the headrest, only to feel the man pluck at her fingers. She tucked her toes inside the chair legs, but the woman kicked at her ankles. Inniki caught a breath of stale cabin air, the sweat and assorted fungal spores from shoes, socks and bare feet, as the female officer gripped the back of her head and stuffed her face towards the floor. Inniki swore at another belt of pain that zoned through her midsection. The male officer told her to *watch her mouth*, that *everything she said could be used against her*. It occurred to Inniki that she was under arrest. It wouldn't be the first time, not that they would know that, but there was usually a good reason. But in the cramped confines of the aircraft cabin, it seemed that Inniki was being arrested for standing up.

Times had changed in Greenland since she had been away.

The pain caught hold of Inniki, and she fought for air to clear her head as the two officers – IGA or the U.S. Immigration and Customs Enforcement – carried her out of the cabin and down the steps of the aircraft to the tarmac apron. Inniki almost laughed at the officers' acronym: *ICE* – there was plenty of that already in Greenland. And now there was more. She wondered if they just as unyielding, if the agency covered as much of the country as its namesake?

The officers tilted Inniki onto her feet as a black SUV, tyres screeching, swerved around the aircraft on the apron and jolted to a stop in front of them. The female officer clamped her hand on

Inniki's head as the man cuffed her wrists behind her back. They opened the back door of the SUV and stuffed her inside. It had taken less than two minutes from the moment they engaged her inside the cabin, to the second the SUV driver hit the gas. Regardless of the wait inside the cabin, Inniki couldn't remember having ever exited an aircraft so quickly. She would have smiled, again, if it wasn't for the pain and that growing feeling of indignance laced with spasms of muscle memory from her youth – a call to action.

"Resist," she breathed even though her aging body shivered at the thought of it.

The driver stomped on the brakes outside a rolling door, waiting for it to rise so that he could drive beneath it. He peered over the steering wheel, tapping it with his fingers, clicking his tongue, and then accelerating forwards as soon the bottom of the door cleared the roof of the SUV. Inniki slid into the back of the front seats as the driver stomped on the brakes a second time.

Then the doors opened.

Then she was pulled out.

Inniki couldn't remember feeling the blood drip out of her, but one of the guards noticed, swapping a crass joke with his partner about *period bleeding* and *should have worn a thicker pad*. She could have responded, could have told them that she understood English, but Inniki stayed silent as they marched her through the door that separated the vehicle bay from the offices and interview rooms. They pushed Inniki through a second door and into the first interview room, unshackling her wrists in favour of another set of cuffs with a longer chain, wound through a loop in the surface of the table. They sat her down and Inniki rested her hands on the table.

Resist, she thought.

"Someone will be here in a minute," said one of the men, tapping the large face of the watch on his wrist. He pointed at the clock on the wall, and then repeated, "One minute." He held up one finger, waiting for Inniki to respond before giving up with a huff. The two guards left the room, shutting the door behind them.

Time, they were obsessed with it. Everything had to happen so quickly. There was no time to react, no time to reflect, there wasn't even time to communicate. And now, in the interview room, the man had pointed to his watch, then pointed at the clock on the wall, as if time was important. It had to be observed. It mustn't be wasted.

Inniki thought about the ice sheet covering Greenland, how the tourist boats in Ilulissat gave their customers a stiff drink with chipped ice from the glaciers. Ice which had travelled for thousands of years, only to calve where the ice met the sea, to be fished up from the black waters in a cloth net, stabbed and chipped into ragged cubes that popped with ancient air when whisky was splashed over them. A thousand years reduced to the pop and crack of air inside a chilled glass. The tourists would be the first to agree, that some things are worth waiting for. And yet, so far, in this new Greenland, everything had to happen yesterday.

There was more blood on the front of Inniki's beige trousers and she shook her head at her choice of clothes, and then chastised herself for blaming herself. She could have walked off the aircraft. She didn't have to bleed.

"You're bleeding?" said a man, as soon as he stepped into the interview room. "Do you need medical attention?" Inniki stared at him and he sighed, poking his head around the door and shouting along the hall for an interpreter.

"I understand English," Inniki said, deciding to resist through dialogue instead of silence.

"You do?"

"Yes."

"And my last question?" The man stepped into the room and shut the door.

"I had an operation recently. Your guards..." Inniki paused. "Is this conversation being taped?"

"Yes," the man said, pointing at the two cameras covering the room. "Audio too."

"Your guards," Inniki continued, "made me bleed when they shoved me to the floor."

"That can happen when people resist arrest."

"I was standing up," Inniki said, as the man sat down on the other side of the table.

"You were told to sit. You didn't." He shrugged.

Inniki folded one hand over the other and leaned back in her seat. She studied the man, noting his youth – about thirty years younger than she was – and the stern cut of his chin. He was clean-shaven and the hair at the sides of his head was trimmed, if a little thin. She had met his type before – been interviewed by them – and imagined that it was just a matter of time before they discovered that she had a history with law enforcement, albeit many years ago.

Time, she thought. *Then and now.*

"I'll get right to it," the man said. "This is your first time in Greenland…"

"I was born in Greenland."

The man shook his head and snorted. "Since the change in circumstances."

"Circumstances?"

"Since the United States took on the stewardship of Greenland, and its people."

"You call this…" Inniki rattled the chain securing her to the table. "This is *stewardship*?"

"The control of your borders has been way too lax for way too long," he said. "You didn't even need a passport to get out of the country."

"To visit *Denmark*."

"That's what I said. *Out of the country*."

"Greenland is a part of the Danish territories."

"It was owned by…"

"We're not *owned by*. Greenland is autonomous. It has self-rule, working towards independence."

"Really? How's that going for you?" The man laughed. "As for autonomous. I think it's best you accept our stewardship and embrace your future. Although," he said, nodding at Inniki's cuffs. "This isn't the best start."

"I was standing up," Inniki said.

"In defiance of a direct order." The man slapped the table. "You need to wake up. I would have thought a woman of your years would understand change – you've seen such a lot of it."

Inniki sank into her seat, tugging her hands as close to her lap as the chain allowed. "Are you baiting me?" she said. "Are you trying to make me angry?"

"Are you angry?"

"What if I am? What's the point?"

The man ignored her. He reached into the breast pocket of his shirt and pulled out a passport. Inniki recognised it as her own.

"You are one of the Greenlanders who do possess a passport." He turned it, holding it in such a way that Inniki understood he was comparing her photo with her face, before reading her name aloud. "Inniki Rasmussen."

"Yes."

"I ran your name as soon as they brought you in. It didn't take long for a whole tonne of interesting stuff to turn up. My colleague is trawling through it now. She'll be along in a minute. I just wondered if there was anything you wanted to say before we begin?"

"Begin what?"

"Processing you so that we can decide what to do with you."

"I just want to go home."

"Don't we all," he said, and sighed. "Of course, it's not that easy when you create problems for yourself."

"I was standing up."

"You were told to sit."

"This is my country. No-one tells anyone to

sit."

"No? Then there's your problem, right there. No discipline. No rules. No order."

"Are you talking about me, or my country?"

The man didn't answer, and neither did he have to. Inniki understood. She'd seen it before. Europeans – mostly Danes – struggling to understand why the Greenlanders didn't do what they expected them to do? Failing to understand that autonomous was another word for separate, self-governing, and that it wasn't just the country that was autonomous, but its people too. A different culture, a different way of life, a different way of living.

"What happens now?" Inniki asked.

"To you or your country?"

Inniki thought for a second, realised that she couldn't separate the one from the other, and opened her mouth to speak, only to stop when the door clicked open, and two people joined them.

"This is my colleague," the man said, as the woman sat down beside him.

Inniki stared past her and focused on the Greenlandic police officer who found a spot to lean against the wall. "And who's he?" she asked.

"Constable David Maratse," said the police officer.

"You're a Greenlander."

"*Iiji*," he said, as he tucked his hands into his pockets.

Part 4

"Ms. Rasmussen," the woman said. "My name is Harper. And this," she said, opening a folder on the table, "is your file. It took a while to print out, which is why my colleague had to start without me."

Inniki turned her head from Harper to her colleague, then back to Maratse, leaning against the wall. It looked like he would light a cigarette at any moment. It had been a long time since Inniki had smoked, but she could suddenly taste tobacco on her tongue, and a phantom trail of the familiar scent tickled the inside of her nose. The thought of smoking overruled the other thoughts swirling around her head, if only for a moment.

"Do I have your attention?" Harper asked.

"Yes."

"Only, it seemed like I didn't there, for a second."

"Can I have a cigarette?"

"No."

Harper flicked through the folder and then closed it, resting her arms on the table. Like her colleague, she was younger than Inniki, but older than the guards who had carried Inniki off the plane.

"When you were in your twenties," Harper said, "you visited America."

"I was twenty-three."

"You were working."

"Yes."

"Who was your employer?"

The chain linking Inniki's wrists rattled as she pointed at the folder. "You have my file."

"I do," Harper said, dipping her chin to look at Inniki. "But I want to hear you say it."

"Okay," Inniki said and sighed. "I was working for Danish intelligence."

"Police intelligence?"

"Yes."

"And you assisted with an American operation?"

Inniki shuddered at the memory, and then pushed it to one side with a flick of her head. "Not really."

"But you were involved?"

"Yes."

"And since your return to Greenland…"

"That's nearly fifty years ago." Inniki glanced at Maratse, wondering if he had read her file also.

"On your return," Harper said, tapping the folder as she continued. "You were involved with a number of activist groups."

"We were fighting for a better future," Inniki said.

"And now?"

"Now *what*?"

"Are you still fighting?" Harper slid the folder to her colleague before continuing, "This kind of thing doesn't help your naturalisation."

"My what?"

"Naturalisation, the process of bringing you back to the country."

"I am back."

"We want to help you settle in."

"I'm settled," Inniki said. She shook her head as she looked from one American to the other. "I have a house – I own it. I have a pension."

"And you've just been to Denmark for surgery."

"For an operation, yes." Inniki forgot all about resisting as she tried to anticipate where the conversation was leading. But it was difficult. It was as if they were stating the facts without using them – simply mentioning them, as if the facts themselves were the problem.

"Who paid for your medical care?"

"The government," Inniki said. "Like they always do."

"And the transport? Your food and lodgings prior to the procedure?"

"The government." Inniki shook her head. "I don't understand."

"No, neither do we. But these things are changing, and it's our job – the job of the IGA…"

"What's that?"

"The office of Intermediary Greenlandic Affairs," Harper said. "In other words, we're the transition team."

"Transition?"

41

"Easing the process of stewardship."

Inniki tried a different tack to make sense of it all. "You mean changing everything to your way of doing things?"

"A more efficient way, yes."

"That's a huge job."

"Not really," Harper said. "After all, the population of Greenland can fit inside Dodger Stadium."

"What's that?"

"A baseball stadium. It's in Los Angeles, California." Harper nodded when her colleague leaned closer to whisper in her ear. He stood up a second later and Inniki watched him leave. "My colleague is going to find you a doctor."

"I'm better now."

"Still," Harper said. "He'll find you a doctor." She paused at a knock on the door. "That'll be the water. Are you thirsty?" she asked, as a young officer carrying four bottles of water entered the room.

"Yes," Inniki said.

Harper nodded for the officer, a neatly trimmed man, to give Inniki one of the bottles. He set the others on the table and left. Harper offered one to Maratse, but he declined. Inniki took a swig of water, then another. She watched Maratse as Harper talked, listening to the American with just one ear as she wondered what Maratse's role was. *Perhaps he's here to arrest me?* She glanced at Harper. *Rather him than them.* She took another swig of water, and then concentrated on what Harper was saying.

"…you're well educated. You speak three languages. I would have thought you would understand why this has to happen. Especially with your background and your history working in intelligence."

"I didn't work for them for very long," Inniki said, screwing the cap back on the bottle. "And it was a long time ago."

"And yet, given your background, surely you must understand the reasons why the US is interested in Greenland? You understand the risks?"

"Risks?"

"To national security. And not just the threat from the air," she said. "As the ice melts the sea lanes open…"

"I didn't think the American government believed in climate change?"

A smile twisted Maratse's lips for a second when Inniki caught his eye. She decided that if she was going to be arrested, she would make sure he was the one to do it.

"That's a naïve comment," Harper said. "One man isn't a government."

"Or woman," Inniki said.

"Yes, if or when that happens."

It was the *when* that caught Inniki's attention, and she decided to give Harper hers.

"Regardless of the incident on the airplane, Ms. Rasmussen." Harper continued. "I'm willing to give you the benefit of the doubt. If we can reach an agreement?"

"What kind of agreement?"

"We can come back to that. Right now, my main concern is your physical health. Once we have established that, we can take the necessary steps to address the contents of your file, and to determine your future."

"What about my future?"

At a knock on the door, Harper lifted her finger for Inniki to wait, calling out *two minutes*. She turned back to Inniki, and said, "That's the doctor. He's going to examine you…"

"Here?" Inniki stiffened. "I don't need an examination."

"Following your examination, we will conduct a thorough interview to decide if you are to remain in Greenland…"

"It's my home…"

"Or," Harper said, lifting her finger again. "Or if it would be better for you to spend the rest of your retirement in Denmark, as a Danish citizen. We have that option," she said. "It's a security clause, written into the stewardship papers."

"A security clause?" Inniki shook her head. "I don't understand."

She twisted in her seat as the doctor entered the interview room. He nodded at Harper before turning to address Inniki.

"I understand you have some pain?"

"I just had an operation. I'm recovering."

"Ah," he said, with another nod at Harper. "Then that explains the bleeding."

"Bleeding?" Inniki looked down at her trousers. She *knew* she had bled, but it bothered her that everyone else was talking about it. Together with the folder on the table – now in Harper's hands as she stood up – it was all too much.

"I'll examine you now," the doctor said.

"*Naamik!*" The feet of Inniki's chair scraped across the floor and the chain between her wrists rattled as she pushed back, positioning her feet ready to lash out, to kick and fight until she had no fight left.

"You're going to have to speak English," Harper said, raising her voice as she moved around the other side of the table.

The doctor advanced towards Inniki's feet. He wore the look of someone who had tried this before, wary but determined. "We just want to help you," he said.

"*Naamik!*" Inniki repeated, drawing back her foot.

"This isn't helping," Harper said. She clicked her fingers, waving two guards from the corridor into the room. The two men bumped around the table, flanking the doctor.

"*Tassa!*" Maratse said, as he pushed away from the wall. "That's enough. She said *no*. Now back off."

"Back off?" Harper said. "Constable, do you really think you have the authority to tell us what to do?"

"I'm a Greenlandic police officer," he said. "She's Greenlandic. I have the authority." Maratse's hand drifted to the butt of the pistol holstered at his hip.

Harper caught the movement and shook her head. "That," she said, "is not wise."

Inniki kept her body facing the doctor, her foot poised to strike, as she flicked her gaze from one American to the next, to Maratse, and then back to the doctor. The room seemed suddenly small, charged as it was with the increasingly sharp tang of adrenaline. The doctor was the first to back down, as he took a step away from Inniki, gesturing at her body with a casual wave of his hand.

"She says she's just out of hospital? What she needs most is rest."

"Doctor?" Harper said.

"I prescribe rest. In fact," he said, nodding at Maratse. "I suggest you place her in the Constable's care and send her home for a week. You can pick up your interview after that."

"That's not your decision to make, Doctor," Harper said.

"No?" The doctor laughed. The look on his face made Inniki think that it wasn't the first time his decision had been challenged. "I think you'll find that the care of the patient..."

"Suspect."

"Patient first, suspect later," the doctor said, batting Harper's comment to one side with another wave of his hand. "Her well-being falls under my jurisdiction. I have the authority to determine whether or not, and *when*, you can continue your interview. I say she needs a week."

Harper drummed her fingers against her thigh, and then nodded for the two guards to stand down. She told them to wait in the corridor, as she stared at the doctor. "One week?"

"Yes."

"And she'll be fit for interview?"

"She'll be more comfortable, I'm sure."

"All right," Harper said, with a curt nod of her head. "One week." She turned to Maratse and said. "She's under your care, Constable."

"*Iiji*," he said.

"And during that time, I expect her to stay in her house, not to leave the village."

"It's a settlement," Maratse said.

"Okay," Harper said. "She can't leave the *settlement*, and neither can you. I expect your department to find the necessary funds for you to stay there, and to cover the cost of your ticket. *My* department has enough expenses as it is."

Inniki resisted the urge to smirk, as she wondered if the IGA – whoever or whatever they really were – was discovering that everything in the Arctic cost more than one imagined, that budgets, like time, were affected by the weather and the environment in exactly the same way as the people were. She looked at Maratse, swapped a knowing glance, as she imagined he was thinking the exact same thing.

"Is she fit to fly?" Harper asked the doctor.

He looked at Inniki, and said, "Are you in pain?"

"Yes."

"More than before?"

"No."

"Do you have a change of trousers?"

"In my luggage," Inniki said, wondering if it was for her comfort or the comfort of the other passengers that she should change her trousers.

The doctor nodded at Harper. "She can fly," he said, before leaving the room.

"Constable Maratse?" Harper said, as she picked up Inniki's folder. "Today is Wednesday. I expect you to escort Ms. Rasmussen to her home, and to stay with her until Tuesday. I will send a team to come and pick her up, at which point your job will be done."

"You'll send a team?" Inniki said.

"Yes, Ms. Rasmussen." Harper waved the folder in her hand. "Your record requires that I send a team."

"We can't just agree that I come to you?"

"No. That's not acceptable. There's no guarantee that you will show up."

"But I'm not going anywhere."

"Regardless," Harper said. "I'm sending a team." She walked around the desk, pausing at the door to say one more thing, "I advise you not to resist when they come, Ms. Rasmussen. Your future depends upon it." Harper glared at Inniki, waiting for the message to sink in, before turning away and storming out of the room.

Inniki waited for her to leave and for the guards outside to shut the door. She looked at Maratse, rattled the chain, and said, "I hope you have a key."

"*Iiji*," he said, as he opened a pouch on his utility belt.

Part 5

Maratse's coffee was cold when Walcott interrupted him. He put it down on the table and shifted his position. If there had been a window, he would have stared out of it. Walcott sighed as he made a few more notes, before pushing the paper to one side.

"What I don't understand," he said. "What *none* of us really understand is why you don't get it?"

"Get what?" Maratse said.

"This." Walcott waved his arm to encompass the room. "What we're doing here – for you."

"For me?"

"Yes, for you. And for that crazy old lady, Inniki Rasmussen. Why don't you understand that we're the best thing that has ever happened, and ever will happen to Greenland?"

Maratse shrugged. "Maybe you should explain it?"

"Maybe I have to." Walcott unscrewed the lid of the thermos can, tipped the last dregs of coffee into his mug and added a generous spoonful of powdered cream, and another of sugar. "Let me

49

lay it out for you," he said, as he stirred his coffee. "Under Danish rule." He held up his hand as Maratse started to protest. "Let me finish," Walcott said. He took a sip of coffee and continued. "Under Danish rule, your country was stagnating. Sure, there's been a lot of modernisation since they got you out of the turf huts – for one thing, you've got broadband Internet."

"Only in the capital."

"Yeah, okay, but it's coming." Walcott conceded the point with a nod. "But apart from a modern hospital, modern museums, and a beautiful cultural centre, what have you really got, eh? That shopping mall is tiny," he said, pointing in the general direction of Nuuk's city centre. Maratse was fascinated by Walcott's relatively keen directional sense from deep within a square building with very few windows. He nodded that Walcott should continue, that he wouldn't interrupt. "You've got an impressive university, and housing is being modernised, but outside the capital, I ask you, what have you got?"

"Peace," Maratse said.

"Is that what you call it? Peace?" Walcott laughed. "What you've got is a whole chunk of nothing, with no connecting roads, telecom masts that are affected by the weather – disabling your communications. You've got a tonne of people living in tiny houses. They've got no car…"

"They don't need one."

"They've got no life insurance, or insurance

of any kind."

"The state provides for them," Maratse said.

"Oh yeah? And how long is that going to last? How long is the *state* going to fly people around the country for a check-up with the doctor? How long is the *state* going to fly police officers, teachers, dentists, doctors and who knows who else, around the country to service each and every settlement? How long?" Walcott took a breath. "Well, not very long, I can tell you that much. And not my United *States*, I can tell you. I understand that the government of Greenland, together with the Danes, had a secret project to move people from the settlements to the cities. I mean, that makes sense. It's way too expensive to have, what, fifty people, sometimes less, living on a tiny island that can only be reached by helicopter. And not even that if the weather socks in. No, better to get them out of the wilderness, and move them to the city. That's what we're going to have to do, if we've even got a chance at making this whole project viable."

"They don't live in the wilderness."

"They don't? You could have fooled me. These people shit in a bucket, and half the houses collect their water from a pumping station. The electricity is provided with a generator, and when that goes... well. It's just not tenable. Not on my watch." Walcott made a face as he took a sip of coffee. "Cold," he said, before continuing. "Then we've got the other side of the coin – the real reason we're here. All this social stuff, to be honest, Constable, it just gets in the way of the one true purpose Greenland has."

Maratse looked at Walcott, ignoring the pause and his cue to respond, preferring to wait for him to continue, to *tell him how it is*, as Maratse imagined he would say.

"The one true purpose of Greenland is strategic," Walcott said. "When you boil it right down, Constable, that's all it is. You're smart. You know it. Inniki Rasmussen knows it, even if she's playing it down. You both have to agree that in the current climate – physical and political – Greenland's geographical position is its greatest and most important asset. Once the ice melts for real, this island is the only thing between the Russians and North America. Hell, they're here already, just off the east coast. All those tourists visiting that so-called tourist facility on Novaya Zemlya." Walcott shook his head. "How come the tourists are predominantly male, between the ages of twenty and thirty, with a physique that would put you and I to shame? I wonder. The world wonders. I don't mind admitting it, Constable, these guys are Russia's crack troops, right on our doorstep. And what assets did the Danes have to stop them? Three ships, a couple of guys on dogsleds, and a Learjet." He shrugged. "Maybe a couple of other assets, what do I know? But what I *do* know is that they had nothing that could be considered a decent deterrent in the event that the Russians, or even the Chinese, decided to show a little muscle. No, we've got more assets – men and equipment – in Thule, at the air base. It's just a shame it's at the top of the country. We need bases on the east coast, in the south, and in the west. And we're going to get them, just as soon as we sort out the population problem."

"Problem?"

"Yes, it's a problem that there's so few of you, spread so far apart. As soon as we've got you contained, well, then we can get to work. I mean, we've already started the *work*, but you know what I mean?"

Maratse let Walcott continue, letting his thoughts drift as he thought about Inniki, their conversations in Kapisillit, and what happened when Harper sent her team to pick her up. Walcott had called a pause after the first part of Maratse's report. He had yet to ask about the second part. Considering how much energy Walcott was using to get things off his chest, Maratse wondered how much he knew, and if he would look at what happened in Kapisillit as an isolated incident, or as something more problematic, endemic, something that needed to be *contained* before the people got the upper hand? Maratse turned his attention back to Walcott when he heard his name.

"Don't you agree, Constable?"

"Agree?"

"Of course. Come on, man, it makes sense. If we're going to stand up to the Russians, we need to do it with such a display that they really get the message. What use is a deterrent if it doesn't have any teeth?"

"You mean the missiles?"

Maratse remembered reading about them in

the newspaper – batteries of missiles with
overlapping fields of fire had been installed as
one of the first things the United States had done
on acquiring Greenland. The reaction from
foreign states had been overwhelming, drawing
Greenland firmly into the spotlight, to the same
degree that it had when Reagan had announced
the Strategic Defence Initiative programme in the
1980s.

"Yes, the missiles," Walcott said. "And more,
much more. We're just getting started. Which,"
he said, drawing out the word. "Brings us back to
you, and what happened last week."

"In Kapisillit?"

"Yes."

Whatever Maratse might have thought about
the American stewardship of Greenland, he had
put most of his thoughts to one side, choosing
instead to think about how he would spend his
retirement, fishing and hunting, until he could no
longer fish or hunt. Once he was too old to enjoy
the land, the sea, and the ice, Maratse imagined he
would just stop. He would always have his books,
but if he couldn't enjoy being outside, he didn't
imagine there being any purpose to *being*. People
often mistook him for being simple, or not caring.
Proving them wrong wasn't important to Maratse,
because to do that, they would have to understand
how he thought, what made him tick. Maratse
didn't wish that on anybody. It wasn't important.
He wasn't important. And if it was naïve to think
that the American's plans for his country
wouldn't affect him, then he was happy to be

naïve.

Inniki changed that.

She pushed some buttons in Kapisillit. She turned his arguments around. She forced him to *argue*, to take a side and to have an opinion that included the future of all Greenlanders, not just him alone.

"You can't be that naïve," she had said one evening.

"I'd like to be," he had said.

"Too bad. I won't let you."

And she didn't.

A seventy-something Greenlander, only just released from hospital, and barely out of handcuffs, forced Maratse to have an opinion, and not one that just stretched to those people in his care, from one moment to the next. No, she forced him to have an opinion about everybody, from that moment on.

"Period," she had said, smiling at the use of an Americanism.

Walcott rapped the table with his knuckle.

"Constable?"

"*Iiji.*"

"I feel like I keep losing you. Do I have your full attention?"

"*Eeqqi,*" Maratse said. "Not all the time. Sorry."

"Then how about we start again? We've got to the point where you escort Inniki Rasmussen to her village."

"Settlement. Smaller than a village."

"Right," Walcott said. "Another part of the

problem. But we'll get to that. Tell me, Constable, once you arrived, what happened then?"

"She rested."

"For seven days straight?"

"For a few days."

"And after that? When she wasn't resting?"

"We talked."

"You talked?" Walcott nodded. "Harper had one of her assistants provide me with a redacted profile and history of Inniki Rasmussen. There are lots of holes, but I understand that she was quite the radical in her day. Did she convert you, Constable?"

"What?"

"Did she encourage you to revolt? To plot against the United States and to resist our stewardship of Greenland?"

Maratse frowned, wondering if he needed a lawyer to answer that question. It sounded like a very *American* thing to need.

"Constable?"

"I don't think I should answer that," he said.

"Because it's true?"

"Because I think it would get me in trouble."

"David," Walcott said. "Look around you. You're in a room with no windows. You relinquished your pistol and service belt at the door. You're already in a world of trouble. How about you just answer the question? Eh? Just tell me, did Inniki Rasmussen try to convince you to plot against the American government?"

"*Imaqa.*"

"That's a *yes*?"

"It's a *maybe*."

"Okay," Walcott said, folding his arms across his chest. "So, tell me, Constable, did she succeed?"

Maratse thought about Inniki's last moments in Kapisillit. He thought about the other residents, what they did, what Harper's team did, and what he chose to do.

"She made a very convincing argument," he said.

"So, you were convinced?"

"*Iiji.*"

"And you understand the consequences of admitting that you were convinced, by Inniki Rasmussen, to plot against the government of the United States of America?" Walcott paused. "Think carefully now, Constable, before you answer."

"She didn't convince me to plot against the government," Maratse said.

"You're sure?"

"*Iiji.*"

"But a second ago, you said you talked, and that she gave a good argument, or words to that effect. Understand this, Constable, this is a preliminary meeting. What we call a 360. The next meeting after this will very much depend on your answer. So, take your time, take a breath, take a sip of cold coffee, and in your own time, answer the damn question."

"You want to know if Inniki convinced me to plot against the government?"

"Yes," Walcott sighed. "That's it. That's

exactly it."

Maratse shook his head.

"No?"

"Not to plot," Maratse said.

"What then?"

Maratse paused to take a sip of cold coffee. He turned the cup in his hands, and said, "She convinced me to act."

Part 6

The view from the windows of Inniki's house captured Maratse, motionless, stocking feet parted, thumbs tucked into the sides of his utility belt, while Inniki bustled about him in the background. She emptied her suitcase. Maratse tilted his head to follow a raven, watching it land on top of one of the small red shipping containers, the kind that fit inside the larger ones. They were perfect for the settlements and could be lifted by a tractor with forks for the purpose. The raven cawed, drawing Maratse's gaze beyond the containers, past the roads, the grasses, the swathes of gravel and sand, to the mountains running along the fjord, and the bigger ones in the background. Inniki pressed a mug of coffee into Maratse's hand and joined him at the window. They didn't speak for the better part of ten minutes, just sipped their drinks, comfortable in the silence broken only by the caw and croak of the raven.

"This is my first time in Kapisillit," Maratse said.

"It's shrinking," Inniki said. "People are

moving away." She pointed to the west. "Nuuk is at the mouth of the fjord."

"*Iiji.*"

"You're a strange one, Constable." Inniki rested her bottom on the arm of the chair closest to the window, lifting her chin to look at Maratse. "You wear the uniform – it fits you. But I can't help feeling that you would rather be wearing something else."

Maratse grunted, and said, "I like the jacket."

"I can see that." Inniki reached out to scratch at something dry and flaky on Maratse's sleeve. "Fish scales," she said.

"*Iiji.*"

"You're a fisherman?"

"I like to fish."

"But you prefer to hunt?"

Maratse finished his coffee and then nodded towards the mountains in the distance. "I like to be outside," he said.

"Why?"

Maratse raised his eyebrow, curious as to why someone like Inniki would need to ask such a question. Inniki caught his look and laughed.

"I know *why*," she said. "I just want to hear *you* say it."

"Because life is simpler out there," he said. "The wind picks up, so you turn the boat towards the waves, quartering them."

"*Aap.*"

"An iceberg calves, so you turn into *that* wave, because it's bigger."

"And full of ice."

Maratse nodded. "But you know it will pass, if you wait long enough."

"But by then you've already moved on," Inniki said.

"*Imaqa*. Maybe."

They said nothing more. After a few minutes, Inniki pushed off the arm of the chair, drawing a look from Maratse as she stifled a soft curse on her lips. She took his mug into the kitchen. Maratse searched for the raven, and then called out that he was going for a walk. Inniki told him to wait.

"I'll come with you," she said.

They walked through the tiny settlement of Kapisillit. Less than one hundred people lived there. All of them waved at Inniki when they saw her, staring quizzically at Maratse, until Inniki slipped her arm through his, drawing smiles from the women, nods from the men, and cheeky grins and whistles from the children.

"They'll think I caught you in Nuuk."

"*Iiji.*"

"In truth, it's good to hold on."

"You're in pain?" Maratse asked.

"Less than before the operation, but enough. I might curse once in a while, I might complain. Just ignore me."

They walked around the block, past the oil tank, the water tank, the containers, the water pumping station. Inniki pointed out the empty houses, pulling Maratse close so that he could look through the windows. Each house had its merits, and Inniki listed them. That one was the closest to the water but had the saltiest windows. This one was out of the wind, but the shadow of the water tank made the inside dull in the autumn. One was too close to the road but had a window box for flowers.

"I've always wanted a window box," Inniki said.

They passed that house each day on their regular walk through Kapisillit. Maratse found a reason to stop each time – to tie his shoelace, or remove a stone caught in the thick tread of his boots. Inniki smiled, humouring him, teasing him that he might tie his laces faster if he stopped looking at the window box. Maratse shrugged, and, when they were ready, and he had taken one last look, they walked on. Inniki found the crook of Maratse's arm to be agreeable – just the right height for her wrist – and Maratse enjoyed the weight of her touch, lighter than a raven.

They talked long into each evening, letting the late summer light fool them into thinking it was still early, only to joke at the time, pushing dinner plates to one side, drinking bottomless cups of coffee, and then tea. No alcohol. Inniki said she had lost her taste for it.

"And then no-one bothers me for a drink," she said, as a sad light flickered across her eyes. "That's our biggest problem," she said. "Alcohol. Get rid of that, and we might be independent already. But it has made us weak."

"Not all of us," Maratse said.

"No, not all, but many." Inniki shook her head. "Too many."

Maratse carried the plates into the kitchen, ignoring Inniki's protests. He boiled more water in a pan for coffee, leaning against the kitchen units as he waited. There were cracks in the linoleum, scars and nicks on the counter, and the small hole in one of the panes of glass in the kitchen window, could easily have been made by a .22 calibre bullet. But everything was clean. Ordered. The shelves and cupboards could accommodate more of everything, but Inniki said she had what she needed. More things only meant more to clean.

"There's something calming about having little," she said, before pointing out of the window at the mountains and the sea. "Especially when we have so much."

Maratse agreed. He made the coffee, added water and a teabag to the pot, and then slipped outside for a cigarette. They both knew that guarding Inniki, stopping her from running away, was unnecessary, but the walks, the simple meals, and the company helped sustain the illusion. Inniki joined Maratse outside the house. She sat on the top step of the wooden stairs and reached out for Maratse's cigarette. She smoked with the air of someone who used to enjoy it, someone who had stopped for many years, and yet still longed for it, once in a while.

"You're a bad influence on me," she said, as she took a last drag and handed Maratse his cigarette, just as she had done the previous night, and the night before that.

Maratse grinned, blew a cloud of smoke

above his head, and then snuffed the cigarette between his finger and thumb. He tossed the butt into a small pot Inniki had found for the purpose.

"Do you want your coffee outside?" she asked.

"I'll come back inside in a minute," he said.

"It's never a minute." Inniki smiled. "It must be quite a window box you're building."

"I'm not building anything."

"No," Inniki said. "Of course not."

She left him to it, knowing that the coffee would be cold when he returned, but it gave her time to fix the sheets and covers on his fold-up bed. Inniki normally lent the bed out to the neighbours, but they agreed that Maratse could use it for the week. Inniki sat down on it, once she had finished straightening the sheets. Maratse's watch was on the floor, together with an English book he had found on Inniki's shelves. She picked it up, found his ticket stub bookmark just a few pages in, and smiled at his persistence. English was not his strong point, he had said, earlier in the week. Some people might call him stubborn – refusing to give in. But Inniki didn't care. It felt good to have a man in the house again, never mind the reason, she didn't care to think about that.

Maratse finished the window box late Saturday night, and presented it to Inniki early Sunday morning. It was indeed a large window box. They agreed that it could hang on the thick wooden handrail of the steps, just outside the door.

"It's too heavy for the any of the windows."

"*Iiji*," Maratse said. Inniki erased the frown on his forehead with a light kiss on his cheek.

"It's very thoughtful of you, Constable. Now all we need is some dirt."

Maratse nodded, and then walked around the house, pushing the remains of a wooden pallet to one side as he lifted a bucket of soil from the ground. He carried it to the steps and handed it to Inniki.

"Where did you get this?"

"I borrowed it," he said.

"Borrowed?"

Maratse pointed up the short street. "From the house. Up there."

"Constable," Inniki said, resting the bucket on the handrail, "did you steal this soil?"

"I might have."

"From my neighbours?"

"It's possible. But," he said, with a grin. "The house was empty."

Inniki laughed as she scooped handfuls of soil from the bucket and dumped them into the window box. Neither of them mentioned the lack of seeds or plants, the box was enough. It was a start. Inniki put the bucket down and clapped the soil from her hands. She said something about tea, and then hid her face behind her hair as she slipped inside the house. Maratse tidied up, and then followed her inside.

"I'm sorry," she said, as they drank tea at the table. "It's nearly time. They'll be coming soon."

Maratse nodded and then sipped his tea.

"This week," Inniki said, "has been extraordinary."

"How?"

"No urgency. I spent a month in Denmark, waiting for an operation, having the operation, then recovering from it. Every day was a case of hurry up and wait – waiting to be told the date for the operation, rushing then waiting to be seen by the doctor, and then the operation itself. I think the only time I didn't have to rush, the only time I didn't feel like I was waiting, was when they knocked me out, and then the morphine after that."

"You can remember how it felt?"

"Oh, I know morphine," she said, and then paused. "That didn't sound right."

"I don't care," he said with a smile.

"Perhaps you should?"

Maratse put his mug down and frowned, confused as to what he should care about. "The morphine?"

"*Aap*, maybe. And my background. The reason *they* want to interview me." Inniki sighed. "Don't you see what they're doing? They're sorting Greenlanders, like in a sieve. Whatever falls through the holes – and they determine the shape and size of each of them – whatever remains, they'll find a way to dump those people on Denmark. Anyone who might rock the boat, who might say something, anyone who complains or starts a ruckus."

"Ruckus?"

"Trouble," Inniki said. "Once you get rid of

all of them, then the rest will just comply, and allow everything to happen around them." Inniki gripped the mug in her hands. They both heard the soft crack of the porcelain handle as it weakened in her grip. "We're too few, David," she said. "Simply too few. That woman – Harper – said the whole population of Greenland could fit inside a baseball stadium. It seems to me that there's a sense of greediness, that they might think we are greedy. So few people spread over so much land. But it's our way of life. It's what we've always known. Greedy?" Inniki laughed. "I have a window box made out of broken pallets, filled with soil stolen from a neighbour. It's empty, no plants or seeds, because we have none. Maybe that's the real problem? We have so little, and so little need, we're not desirable. We will never consume enough to be desirable. Do you see?"

Maratse shook his head.

"That's because it's alien to you," Inniki said, pointing at him. "Look at you. You brought the clothes you stand up in. I'm guessing, perhaps hoping, that you have a change of underwear, but I know you've worn the same shirt all week. You have a watch and a book by your bed. There's a toothbrush in a glass in the bathroom, and a gun on your belt in the hall." Inniki paused to take a long breath. She shook her head, slowly, as she exhaled. "You have to be careful, David. You've got less than me. You might even *need* less than me. They won't want you here. So, maybe that's our lot. That's our future. We can find a tiny flat in a Danish town and grow seeds in our window box."

"I won't survive in a town," Maratse said, quietly. He looked out of the window and stared at the mountains.

"No," Inniki whispered. "I don't think you will, either. But what will you do about it?"

"What *can* I do about it?"

Inniki put her mug on the table and fiddled with the handle. It crackled between her fingers until she twisted it free of the mug. She put the handle on the table, and said, "You can fight."

Part 7

The helicopter made a pass over Kapisillit before landing in front of the tiny store in a storm of grit and dust. Four men clad in black climbed out of the helicopter and stood to one side as the pilot shut down the engine and applied the rotor brake. The men adjusted their equipment, looked around the settlement, pointing and laughing for a moment, until one of them pulled out a phone, punched in a number and pressed it to his ear.

Maratse moved away from the window at the sound of his mobile ringing in his jacket pocket. His lips flattened into a thin smile as he looked at Inniki.

"I have to take it," he said.

She nodded.

Maratse walked out of the lounge and into the tiny hallway. He dug his hand inside his pocket to pull out the phone, tilting his head to one side as he did so, curious at the sound of something clattering in the kitchen.

"Maratse," he said, as he answered the call.

"Ah, we're here," said a man in English. "Where are you?"

"Just across the road from you." Maratse opened the door of the house and stepped out onto the short wooden deck at the top of the stairs. He raised his arm, and then waved as the man turned one way and then the other. Maratse lowered his hand as one of the men spotted him.

"We see you. Bring her out."

Maratse slipped his phone into his pocket as the man ended the call. He stepped back inside the house, only to duck to one side as Inniki walked out of the lounge with the stock of a hunting rifle tucked into her shoulder, and the barrel pointing straight at Maratse. She pushed past him, working the bolt of the rifle to chamber a round as she stepped out onto the deck.

"Inniki, don't," Maratse said.

She ignored him.

Inniki's first shot slammed into the earth twenty metres in front of the Americans. Her second shot, just ten metres in front of them, sent them scurrying for cover – two behind a small shipping container to the right of Inniki's house, while the two other men slid into the dirt behind a row of three empty oil drums draped with fishing equipment. Maratse's phone rang a second later, just as Inniki stepped back inside the house.

"You can stay, or you can go," she said, holding the rifle in one hand as she reached for the door handle. "I don't mind either way but let me say this before you decide."

"Say what?" Maratse said, as he pulled the phone from his pocket.

"You've been wonderful company this past

week. And if nothing else, it's all been worth it."

"Inniki."

"Stay or go, David. It's decision time."

Maratse looked at the mobile in his hand. He stared at it for a second, before slipping it onto the windowsill. Maratse took one step across the narrow hallway and tugged his utility belt off the hook next to Inniki's coat. He buckled it around his waist, checked his pistol, and then slipped it back into the holster. He nodded at the door as he picked up his mobile. Inniki closed the door, laughing as she pointed at the empty keyhole.

"I don't think I've ever locked it," she said, as Maratse answered the call.

"What the hell is going on?" Maratse moved the phone from his ear as the American agent shouted down the other end.

"Just a minute," Maratse said. He looked at Inniki, and said, "What do you want me to say?"

"Tell them I've decided to stay here."

Maratse nodded, then relayed Inniki's message. The agent's words filled the hallway, interspersed with curses that made Inniki smile, and a string of orders backed up with the threat of reinforcements.

"I mean it, Constable," the man said.

"*Iiji.*" Maratse ended the call and shrugged at Inniki.

"I'll make a pot of tea," she said.

Inniki thumped the rifle onto the dining table before walking into the kitchen. She filled the pan with water, glancing at Maratse as he stepped into the living room, close to the table.

"You can take it if you want," she said, nodding at the rifle. "I've made my point."

"You're not going to use it again?"

Inniki waited for the water to boil, and then dumped two teabags into the pot. "I never intended to shoot anyone," she said, as she carried the pot and two mugs to the table.

"Then why?"

"Because they need to know it's not right. That they can't just do as they please with us. That we actually have a right to be here, to live out our lives in our own homes, if we so choose."

"But shooting at them…"

"Won't change anything, David," Inniki said. "They've made their decision already. If it wasn't for the doctor, they would have *processed* me back there in the airport. He gave me a week, and I've enjoyed it, David. I really have. But it doesn't change anything. I have a history that identifies me as problematic. They will send me to Denmark."

"They'll never let you come back," Maratse said. He choked on the last words, drawing Inniki around the table to take his hand. "It's not right."

"I know."

"You belong here."

"I know," she said. "But look at you." Inniki brushed her thin hand along Maratse's jaw. "We're talking about me, but you're thinking about someone else."

"This is my country," he said.

"Yes."

"Not just a strategic piece of…"

"Real estate?" Inniki smiled. "I know, David."

"*They* don't." Maratse stabbed a finger at the helicopter. He pulled away from Inniki, turned his head towards the window. His hand moved to the grip of his gun and he curled his fingers around it.

"Don't," Inniki said.

"You did."

"I have less to lose." Inniki reached for his hand and began plucking his fingers from his pistol. "Look at me, David. I'm seventy-one years old. I am content with my life. Content with what I have achieved, what I've done – the good and the bad. They can't take that away from me."

"But they can take the land from you. The sea. The ice."

"No," she said. "I carry them here." Inniki took Maratse's hand, placed it flat on her chest. "I'll carry Greenland and its people in here, forever. The worst they can do is send me to Denmark. And then they'll be sorry," she said, squeezing Maratse's hand as she stepped away from him. She pointed at the men scurrying into defensive positions in the dirt outside her house, moving closer, exchanging hand signals. "They're right about one thing – many things, actually."

Maratse flicked his head around to look out of the window as one of the men reached the steps. His hand twitched and he reached for his pistol, drawing it out of his holster.

"Our infrastructure is terrible, and terribly expensive," Inniki said. She walked around Maratse, ignoring his warnings about getting too close to the door. "Our communications are just as costly. Two things that are essential when organising a movement. We discovered this back in the 70s and again in the 80s."

"Inniki," Maratse said. "Move away from the door."

"But I can do more damage from Denmark. I can hurt them from there, make a real nuisance of myself, maybe even inspire a revolt. It just takes a spark, David. One spark and a whole lot of preparation. That's all."

"Inniki."

Maratse let go of his pistol as she stepped into the hall. The front door splintered open a second later. The first agent ducked into the hallway, covering Maratse with his pistol tucked tight to his body, his elbows digging into his belly. The second agent burst past his partner to subdue Inniki, tackling her with his body, bloodying her lip on their way down to the floor as his forehead cracked into her face. Maratse jerked forwards as the air whumped out of Inniki's chest.

"Don't fucking move," the first agent said. "I have you, and I will shoot. Cop or no cop."

"After today," the second agent said, as he scrambled off Inniki, pulling plastic strips from his belt and securing them around her wrists, "he won't be a cop for much longer."

"You have to get with the program, Constable," the first agent said. "You have to understand that this is bigger than you. There are more important things going on than a couple thousand people scratching a living out of the dirt."

"I got her," his partner said.

Maratse bristled as a third man entered the house. Two of the agents dragged Inniki to her feet, tugging her out of the door by her arms, as the first agent covered Maratse with his pistol.

"You need to relinquish your weapon," he said. "Take it out of your holster. Real slow now."

"Boss?"

The first agent tilted his head, as the men outside called to him. "What?"

"You better come out here."

"Just a minute," he said, before stepping back into the hall. He waved his pistol and nodded for Maratse to walk ahead of him, then pulled Maratse's pistol from his holster and tucked it into the front of his belt. "Down the steps and…"

The last words died on the agent's lips as he looked up to see a circle of men, women and children, the residents of Kapisillit. Two of the men and one of the women were armed. One man held his daughter on his hip, an elderly lady sat on a plastic fish crate, her arm clutched around a teenage boy's waist.

"What do we do, boss?"

"I don't know."

"What about the kid with the camera?"

Maratse laughed. All the *kids* had cameras, smartphones, older mobiles, their parents too. It crossed Maratse's mind that these were the people scratching a living from the dirt. These mothers and fathers, sons and daughters. The very old, the very young, and everyone in between.

These were the people of Greenland.

His people.

Inniki twisted within the agents' grip to look at Maratse. The wrinkles of age were gone, smoothed flat and soft by the warm Greenlandic wind blowing down from the mountains, across the sea, stirring up dust and trouble between the grasses and the houses of Kapisillit. She grinned at him, lifting her chin, eyes shining as the wind caught her black hair, shivering the lightning streaks as she stood stall between her captors.

"This is what I mean," she said, in Greenlandic.

"*Iiji.*"

"It's all I could ask for. It's all we need. The start of something bigger than you or me, David. Bigger than all of us."

Maratse nodded. Then stepped forward, pushing past the agents to take Inniki's hands. The men reached for their pistols as Maratse tugged his knife from his utility belt, only to stand down when their boss told them to relax. Maratse cut the plastic ties and put his knife away. He took Inniki's hand, and said, "I'm taking her in."

The first agent nodded and lowered his pistol, just as Maratse led Inniki to the helicopter.

The Greenlanders clumped around them. The children pressed their fingers into Inniki's hands, tugging her away from Maratse, squealing as she kissed their heads, cupping their cheeks, as she gently, insistently, pushed them away, working her way back to Maratse, taking his hand, nodding at the helicopter, leading him when the children blocked his path, letting herself be led when he found a space between them to stretch out, to move forwards. The agents followed them from behind, keeping a wary eye on the Greenlanders with guns, waving to the pilot to start the engines.

"I'll be all right," Inniki said, as they reached the helicopter. Brushing the hair of one of the more persistent children. "But I'll need someone here," she said, turning to Maratse.

"I know," he said.

Inniki smiled as he held out his hand, helping her up, as she clambered into the helicopter. She sat in the middle of the bench seat behind the pilots, grasping Maratse's hand as he sat down beside her.

"You've made your decision then," she said, raising her voice as the engines began to whine.

"*Iiji.*"

"I knew you would," Inniki said.

She closed her eyes and rested her head on Maratse's shoulder. Maratse stared straight ahead, past the pilots, drawn by the icebergs in the fjord and the mountains in the distance. *Some things*, he knew, *were worth fighting for*.

Epilogue

Maratse pictured the mountains beyond the walls of the interview room at the IGA. In a month or so the first dusting of snow would arrive. Before that, Nuuk would be awash in rain, the heavy kind that didn't know when to stop. It was one of the reasons Maratse preferred the far north, the drier, colder climate of the sledge dog districts.

"And I've lost you, again," Walcott said.

"*Iiji*," Maratse said, shaking the image of mountains from his mind, as she turned to look at Walcott. "What happens next?"

"Next?" Walcott clicked his pen in and out, drawing out the moment. "Fortunately for you, your report matched the report of our agents in the field. Ms. Rasmussen will be deported. Under our agreement with the Danes, that window is still open. We'll have her out of the country before the end of the month. As for you." Walcott sighed. "That's pretty much up to you."

Maratse frowned. "I don't understand."

"The truth is we need people like you. Someone who knows the land and its people. Quite frankly, there's some concern that what happened in Kapisillit, could happen again, all over Greenland. Despite what you might think, Constable, we're not monsters. We're also employees. Sure, I stand by everything I said, that when you look at Greenland through American eyes, when you look at the global picture, it's hard to worry about a bunch of people who can fit…"

"Inside a baseball stadium?"

"Right," Walcott said. "Exactly. But there's a bigger picture, Constable. And we're just trying to make the world safe for our children. So," he said, lifting the thermos flask to check if they really had finished all the coffee. He put it down again and looked at Maratse. "So how about you help us look after Greenland's children, and their parents, and their grandparents? How about that? Can you do that?"

"I'm not being fired?"

"Some people in this administration might prefer that you were fired. But the simple fact is that you speak our language, you speak *their* language, and you seem to have this connection with the land, and I think that's what we're missing." Walcott stopped as Maratse laughed. "What?" he said, with a slight shake of his head. "Did I say something funny?"

"You sounded human," Maratse said.

"I *am* human. We all are. Okay," he said. "Some of us are more human than others."

"What do you want me to do?"

"Right, well," Walcott said. He leaned forwards, beckoning for Maratse to do the same.

"We need to organise the people in the villages and the smaller places."

"Organise them?"

"Right. We need someone who can talk to them – in their own language. Someone they will trust. Someone who can give them hope, and," he said, with a bob of his head. "It helps if that person can diffuse any tension, just like you did with Inniki Rasmussen."

"Diffuse the tension?"

"Get rid of the guns," Walcott said, with a wink. "We think you're a good fit, Constable. What do you say?"

"You're going to fly me around the country, to talk to my people?"

"That's right. You'll have your own dedicated chopper. And a team, of course. Administrative and a bit of muscle, if things get difficult."

"Any Greenlanders?"

"Just you, I'm afraid. You'll have to function as a translator too. There might even be a pay bonus for that."

"And I talk to the people?"

"No," Walcott said, raising a finger. He pointed at Maratse's chest. "You *organise* them. Light a fire under them. Give them the spark they need to get moving, and to get motivated," he said.

It was the spark that did it.

Maratse took a breath, nodded once, and said, "*Iiji*. I'll do it."

"Good," Walcott said. He slapped Maratse's arm. "I'll draw up the paperwork. Why don't you hang around for a while, Constable? I'll see if I can rustle up some lunch, and some more coffee. How about that?"

"That would be good."

"That's great." Walcott leaned back in his seat. "I knew you'd come around, Constable. I just knew it."

THE END

Author's Note

While this novella contains a lot of information, snippets of history, and elements of modern day problems in a modern Greenland, it is first and foremost a speculative story. On the day that President Trump announced that he was considering buying Greenland in what he described as a real estate deal, he thrust Greenland into the spotlight. He also pissed a lot of people off. While I never will pretend to be Greenlandic, to fully appreciate the emotions such a statement might arouse, I was frustrated at his bluster. But he does have a point. Strategically, Greenland is hot property, prime real estate for development in the modern race for possession of the Arctic. It makes sense for the United States to increase their presence in Greenland, and it makes sense to cut through any political barriers by just buying the country.

Except, you just don't do that.

Greenland is an autonomous country, with its own government, and its own people: the

Greenlanders. While Denmark has played a huge role in Greenland's history – for better and worse – Denmark doesn't own Greenland, and neither is it for sale.

I usually blame Maratse for many of the novellas I write, but this time it isn't his fault. I convinced Maratse and Inniki Rasmussen (*Narkotika*) to help me tell this story. But it stands apart and alone from any of my Greenland crime and thriller series.

It is also complete fabrication, speculation and bluster. Considering the source of my inspiration, I think it is quite apt.

And yes, the Americans are the so-called *bad guys* in this story. It was their turn.

Chris
November 2019
Denmark

About the Author

Christoffer Petersen is the author's pen name. He lives in Denmark. Chris started writing stories about Greenland while teaching in Qaanaaq, the largest village in the very north of Greenland – the population peaked at 600 during the two years he lived there. Chris spent a total of seven years in Greenland, teaching in remote communities and at the Police Academy in the capital of Nuuk.

Chris continues to be inspired by the vast icy wilderness of the Arctic and his books have a common setting in the region, with a Scandinavian influence. He has also watched enough Bourne movies to no longer be surprised by the plot, but not enough to get bored.

You can find Chris in Denmark or online here:

www.christoffer-petersen.com

By the same Author

THE GREENLAND CRIME SERIES
featuring Constable David Maratse
SEVEN GRAVES, ONE WINTER Book 1
BLOOD FLOE Book 2
WE SHALL BE MONSTERS Book 3
INSIDE THE BEAR'S CAGE Book 4

Short Stories from the same series
KATABATIC
CONTAINER
TUPILAQ
THE LAST FLIGHT
THE HEART THAT WAS A WILD GARDEN
QIVITTOQ
THE THUNDER SPIRITS
ILULIAQ
SCRIMSHAW
ASIAQ
CAMP CENTURY
INUK
DARK CHRISTMAS
POISON BERRY

CHRISTOFFER PETERSEN

NORTHERN MAIL
SIKU
VIRUSI
BAIT
THE WOMEN'S KNIFE
ICE, WIND & FIRE

and

THE GREENLAND TRILOGY
featuring Konstabel Fenna Brongaard
THE ICE STAR Book 1
IN THE SHADOW OF THE MOUNTAIN Book
2
THE SHAMAN'S HOUSE Book 3

and

THE DARK ADVENT SERIES
featuring Police Commissioner Petra "Piitalaat"
Jensen
THE CALENDAR MAN Book 1
THE TWELFTH NIGHT Book 2
INVISIBLE TOUCH Book 3
NORTH STAR BAY Book 4

and

THE POLARPOL ACTION THRILLERS
featuring Sergeant Petra "Piitalaat" Jensen *and
more*
NORTHERN LIGHT Book 1
MOUNTAIN GHOST Book 2

and

UNDERCOVER GREENLAND
introducing Inniki Rasmussen *and* Eko Simigaq
NARKOTIKA Book1

and

THE DETECTIVE FREJA HANSEN SERIES
set in Denmark and Scotland
FELL RUNNER Introductory novella
BLACKOUT INGÉNUE Book 1

and

MADE IN DENMARK
short stories featuring Milla Moth *set in Denmark*
DANISH DESIGN Story 1

and

THE WHEELMAN SHORTS
short stories featuring Noah Lee *set in Australia*
PULP DRIVER Story 1
and

THE WILD CRIME SERIES
featuring wildlife biologist Jon Østergård
set in Denmark and Alaska
PAINT THE DEVIL Book 1
LOST IN THE WOODS Book 2
CHERNOBYL WOLVES Book 3

and

GREENLAND NOIR (POETRY)
inspired by Seven Graves, One Winter & more
GREENLAND NOIR Volume 1

and

GUERRILLA GREENLAND
featuring Constable David Maratse
ARCTIC STATE
ARCTIC REBEL

and

THE BOLIVIAN GIRL
a hard-hitting military and political thriller series
THE BOLIVIAN GIRL Book 1

and

CAPTAIN ERRONEOUS SMITH
featuring CAPTAIN ERRONEOUS SMITH
THE ICE CIRCUS Book 1

and

GREENLAND MISSING PERSONS
featuring CONSTABLE PETRA JENSEN
THE BOY WITH THE NARWHAL TOOTH
THE GIRL WITH THE RAVEN TONGUE
THE SHIVER IN THE ARCTIC
THE FEVER IN THE WATER

Made in the USA
Las Vegas, NV
05 August 2022